To Heidi,
with love from Mummy xxx

M. R.

To my sister Jessica,
who has a wonderful smile xx

B. M. S.

Text copyright © 2019 by Michelle Robinson • Illustrations copyright © 2019 by Briony May Smith • All rights reserved. No part of this book may be reproduced, transmitted, or stored in an information retrieval system in any form or by any means, graphic, electronic, or mechanical, including photocopying, taping, and recording, without prior written permission from the publisher. • First U.S. edition 2019 • Library of Congress Catalog Card Number pending • ISBN 978-1-5362-0939-6 • This book was typeset in Walbaum. The illustrations were done in pencil and colored digitally. • Candlewick Press, 99 Dover Street, Somerville, Massachusetts 02144 • visit us at www.candlewick.com Printed in Humen, Dongguan, China • 19 20 21 22 23 24 APS 10 9 8 7 6 5 4 3 2 1

TOOTH FAIRY
in Training

Michelle Robinson

illustrated by

Briony May Smith

CANDLEWICK PRESS

My tooth fairy training starts today!
I'm learning from my sister, May.

May says, *"First thing fairies do is practice the old switcheroo.*

Lift the pillow,
look beneath . . .

leave the coins . . .

and take the teeth.

Do it well and
you're a keeper.

*One rule, Tate:
don't wake the sleeper."*

So I go gently.

Piece of cake!

May says,
"Now do it . . .

in a lake."

This baby hippo
needs a visit.

Not every child's a
human, is it?

"Careful," May says, *"some kids bite.*
Quick, Tate, we haven't got all night!"

I dry my wings
for visit two.

May says, *"Not the kangaroo.*

Your next tooth's waiting down that trail...."

I duck and dodge the mother's tail.

"Come on!" May says . . .

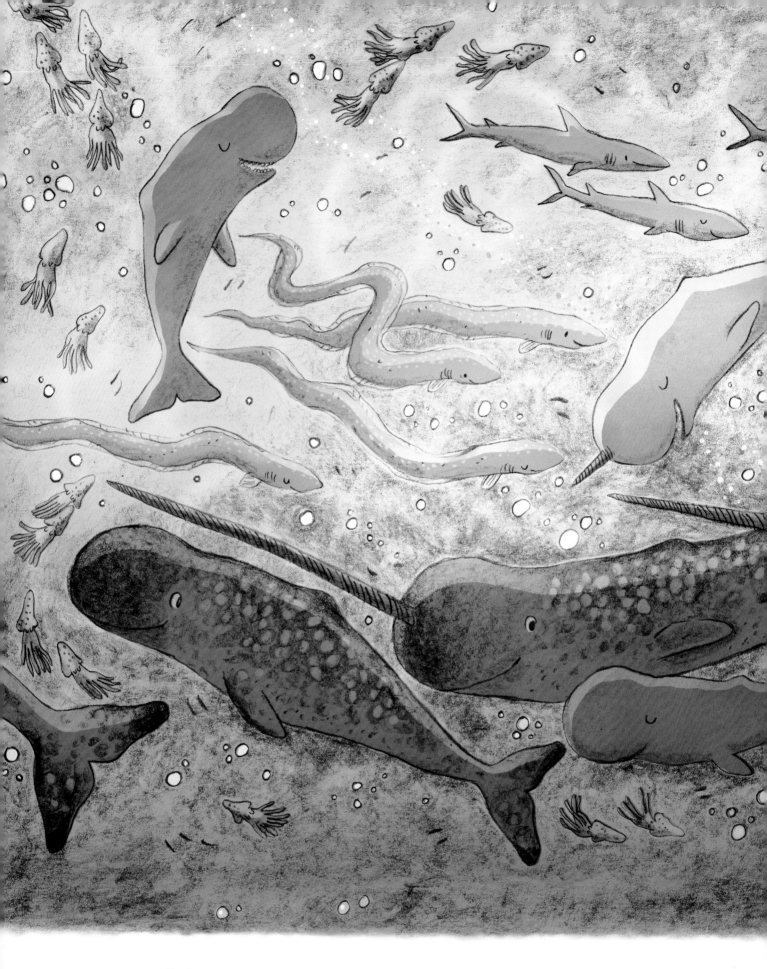

and down we go. *"Watch out for the undertow!"*

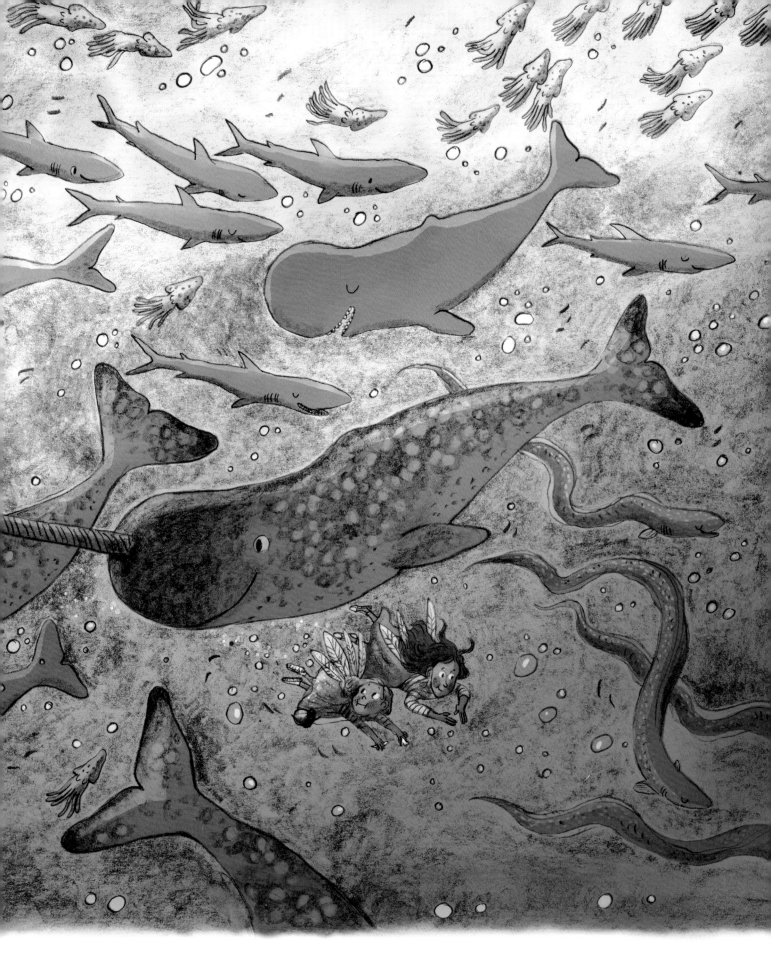

Squid, shark, narwhal, conger eel. *"Up next,"* May says . . .

"a fluffy seal."

I ask, *"This one?"* May says, *"The other."*

Oh, dear — I think she means its brother.

It can't get worse than *that* now, can it?
We've almost flown around the *planet*.

Just a gentle
jungle wander . . .

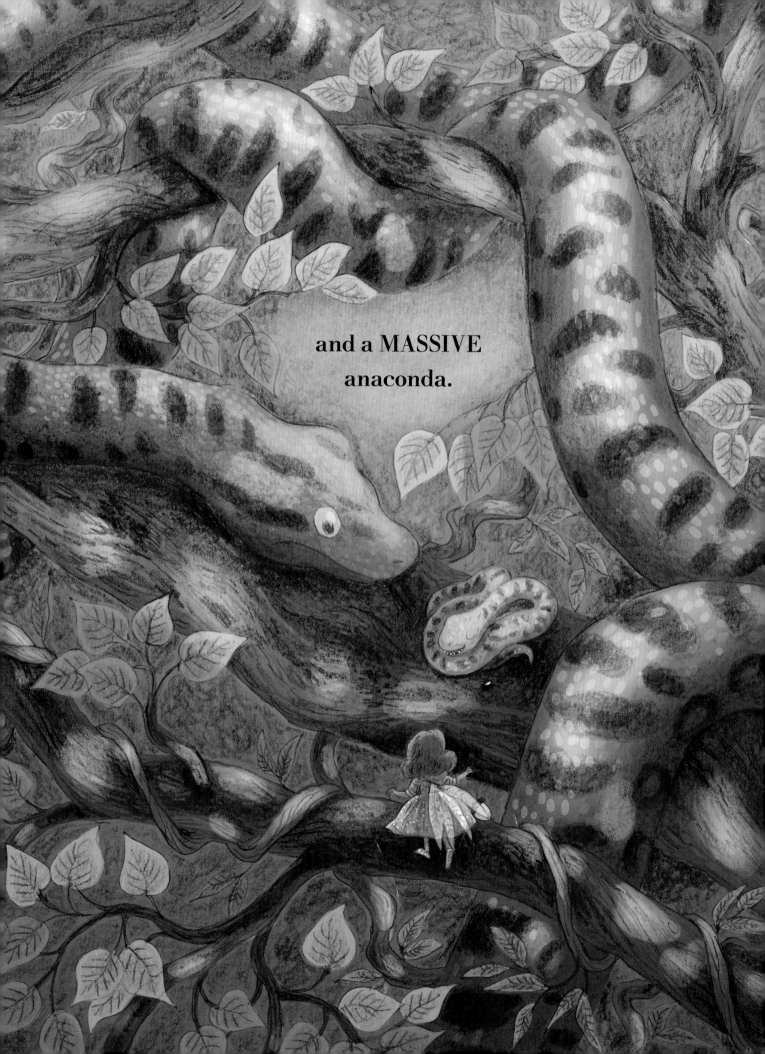

and a MASSIVE anaconda.

Snakes lose teeth as well,
you know.

"And swallow fairies,"
May says. *"GO!*

*Well done, Tate.
Snake teeth are rare.*

*One final tooth, then
home, I swear."*

A little girl.
I can't go wrong.

But hang on—
where's my money gone?

CLANG!

Oh, no! She woke up! OW!

May says, *"We're in trouble now!"*

Of all the teeth!
Of all the kids!
The sharks! The crocs!
The giant squids!

I had to get caught
by *Melissa* . . .
a doll-collecting
fairy kisser.

I flap my wings. I make a wish.

I give my magic wand a SWISH!

Before Melissa knows what's hit her . . .
I've covered her in sleepy glitter.

Home at last, May's proud of me.
"You did it by yourself." Yippee!
Tooth Fairy Tate! I passed the test!
But even *fairies* need their rest.

It's lights-out time in Fairy Town.

May whispers as I snuggle down,
"We'll fetch more teeth tomorrow night—
Melissa lost one more! Sleep tight!"